The Case of the
Rainy Day Mystery

Read all the Jigsaw Jones Mysteries

The Case of the
Rainy Day Mystery

by James Preller
illustrated by Jamie Smith
cover illustration by R. W. Alley

A
LITTLE APPLE
PAPERBACK

SCHOLASTIC INC.
New York   Toronto   London   Auckland   Sydney
Mexico City   New Delhi   Hong Kong   Buenos Aires

For David, Harriet, Julia, and Owen

— J.P.

ISBN 0-439-42631-6

12 11 10 9 8 7 6 5 4 3 2 1   3 4 5 6 7 8/0

Printed in the U.S.A.   40
First printing, June 2003

CONTENTS

Chapter One
Joey

Saturday, 10:00 A.M.

Joey Pignattano stood on my front doorstep.

In the pouring rain.

And dripped water from his nose to his toes.

Plip, plink, plop.

"Quick, Jigsaw," Joey said. "Let me in!"

So, quickly, I let him in. His cheeks were flushed red.

"What are you up to, Joey?" I asked.

Joey looked puzzled. "I'm up to about

four feet, three inches. The same as yesterday."

"I don't mean what height you're up to, I mean what are you *doing*," I tried to explain.

"Doing?" Joey asked, still confused. "I'm talking to you, Jigsaw."

"I *know* you're talking to me, Joey," I answered. "What I meant was . . . oh, forget it!"

"Forget what?" he wondered.

"Forget I asked anything."

"I can't even remember *what* you asked!" Joey exclaimed. "How am I supposed to forget it?"

"You'll find a way," I answered with a sigh.

Joey slipped off his wet boots. A puddle formed on the floor. Joey did not take off his raincoat. My dog, Rags, kept circling Joey, sniffing at his belly.

Joey tried to gently push away Rags with his left hand. He kept his right arm pinned to his side. "Scoot, Rags, scoot."

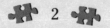 2

I suggested we go down to my basement office.

I took a seat at my desk. A sign behind it read JIGSAW JONES, PRIVATE EYE.

"I'll ask again, Joey," I said. "What are you up to? I can tell that it's some kind of trouble."

Joey blinked. "You can?"

"You're hiding something under your raincoat," I said. "Food, I'd guess. And probably," I continued, "food that you're not supposed to have."

Joey's mouth opened in surprise. "How did you know?" he asked.

"I'm a detective, Joey. It's my job to be observant."

"Ob-ser-who?"

"*Observant*," I repeated. "It means I look at things closely."

Joey nodded as if he understood. I had my doubts. Meanwhile, he unzipped his raincoat. Joey pulled out a crumpled

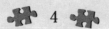

shopping bag. "I need help with something," Joey said. "But first you have to tell me. How did you know I was up to something?"

"Your face was red when you came to the door," I told him. "And you were puffing for air. That told me you had been running."

"Maybe I ran for the fun of it," Joey said.

"Maybe," I said. "But that wouldn't explain two things. First, your boots were on the wrong feet."

Joey smacked the side of his head. "Oh! So that's why I tripped so much!"

"Second, there was a bulge under your raincoat," I explained. "You had your arm pinned to your side. I knew you were hiding something under there."

Joey smiled. "Wow, you are ob-ser . . . ver, er, something-or-other."

"Observant," I corrected. "Rags told me it was food."

"Rags *told* you?" Joey asked.

"Rags has a nose for food," I told Joey.

"In fact, food is pretty much all Rags ever thinks about. He's like you that way, Joey. Rags kept poking his nose into your raincoat."

I pointed at the brown bag. "What's in there, Joey?"

Chapter Two

Stashing the Loot

Joey's eyes twinkled. "Here's the best snack food in the world," he answered happily.

Joey pulled out a squished box of Hostess Twinkies. "Golden delicious cake on the outside," he said. "Yummy cream filling inside!"

"It looks soggy and squished," I noted.

Joey shrugged. "I told you I tripped on my way over here. I guess I smushed them when I fell in that puddle."

I grinned. "You fell in a *poodle*?"

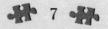

"A poodle?"

"Yeah," I joked. "It's been raining cats and dogs. You fell in a poodle." I smiled hopefully at Joey.

Joey blinked, blank-faced.

"Get it?" I prodded. "A poodle . . . not a puddle. You know, raining *cats* and *dogs*. Stepped in a *poodle*. It's a joke, Joey."

"Not a very funny one," he said.

"I guess not," I agreed.

"Anyway," Joey said, "I need a detective, Jigsaw. Not a comedian."

"Sure, Joey. What's the problem?"

Joey pushed the soggy box of Twinkies toward me across the desk. "I want you to hide them from me."

"Huh?"

Joey explained that he secretly bought the Twinkies with his allowance. "But my mother doesn't like me to eat junk food," Joey confessed. "If she found out, she'd take them away."

"So you want me to hold on to them?" I asked.

Joey nodded. "Yeah, and, well, maybe I'll come by every day and eat a couple."

"That's the job?" I asked. "You want Jigsaw Jones, private eye, to hide a box of Twinkies?"

"Yep."

"Why don't you hide them yourself?" I wondered. "Why ask me?"

Joey frowned. "If I have them in my house, I won't be able to stop eating," he told me. "I'd eat all twelve Twinkies at one time, and then I'd probably hurl."

"Hurl?" I asked.

"You know," Joey said. "Hurl, vomit, throw up, toss my cookies . . ."

"I get it," I said.

Joey continued, warming to the subject. "Blow chunks, heave, spew . . ."

"Joey, enough! I GET IT!" I yelled.

"Okay, I'll do it," I decided. "Even if it does sound a little crazy."

"Are you going to call Mila?" Joey asked.

"I don't need my partner for this one," I replied. "Besides, Mila missed school on Friday. I think she might be sick."

Joey nodded.

"This job will cost you a dollar," I told him.

Joey gulped. "A dollar? That's too much, Jigsaw. How about if I pay you in Twinkies?"

"I don't work for peanuts, and I don't work for Twinkies, either," I replied.

Joey sighed. "I don't have a dollar, Jigsaw. I spent my extra change on Reese's peanut butter cups."

"Nice breakfast," I noted.

Joey agreed that it was.

"Okay, Joey," I said. "We'll figure out the payment later on." I rose from my seat.

"Um, Jigsaw?" Joey said. "There's just one thing."

"Yeah, what's that?"

Joey rubbed his belly. "Can I eat a couple of Twinkies now? I'm awfully hungry."

Chapter Three

Chicken Pox

I went to see Mila on Sunday morning.

Her stepmom, Alice, answered the door. Alice was tall and slim, with flowing blond hair.

"Mila isn't feeling well," Alice said.

"I figured," I answered. "Can I say hello?"

"Mila has chicken pox," Alice told me.

"Bummer," I said. "I had chicken pox in kindergarten. I scratched for four days."

Alice laughed. "Let me check with Mila. She's been sleeping on and off all morning."

Alice's long legs carried her up the stairs

in twos. She was back faster than you could say, "April showers bring May flowers."

"Please make it a short visit," Alice said. "Mila needs her rest."

I started up the stairs.

"And Jigsaw?" she called after me. "Mila is feeling very . . . *sensitive*. Don't say anything about her face."

I nodded, since nodding seemed like the thing to do. Why would I say anything about Mila's face?

I knocked gently on Mila's door and went inside. Her parents had wheeled a television into her room. *SpongeBob SquarePants* flickered on the screen. Mila was propped up in bed, leaning on a bunch of pillows. She stared at the wall.

"Hi, Mila," I said to her back.

"Harrumph." She didn't turn to face me.

"You feeling okay?"

"No," Mila groaned. She said something else, but I couldn't understand it.

"What?" I asked. "I can't hear you, Mila. Stop talking to the wall."

"I'm NOT feeling okay," Mila said louder. She still didn't turn to look at me.

"Mila," I said. "I'm your partner. How bad is it?"

"You won't laugh?"

"No, I won't laugh," I promised.

Then Mila turned around.

And it was a hard promise to keep.

Her face was covered in red dots. Her

nose, her chin, even her eyelids — tiny red scabs everywhere.

I hate to say this, but I'd seen better-looking faces on pizza pies.

"Pretty gross, huh?" Mila whispered.

I paused. It's always best to be honest — but not always right away. So I lied. "You look . . . just fine," I managed to say.

"Jigsaw!" Mila shouted. "Look at my face! It's a big scab."

"You look . . . pretty," I said.

"Pretty disgusting," Mila replied.

I put my hands in my pockets.

And just stood there.

"We've got a new case," I finally said. "Lucy Hiller just called me. I have to go to her house now."

Mila nodded.

"I don't suppose you can help?" I asked.

Mila turned away, burying her face in the pillow. "Murphfff-dimffft," she said.

How could I argue with that?

I left a few minutes later. This was one case I'd have to solve alone.

Chapter Four

Lucy

Being a detective is like being a mail carrier. You have to work in rain, sleet, or snow.

Today, there was rain.

Lots of it.

Coming down in buckets.

I rode my bike through the pouring slop. Rain beat down on my windbreaker — *flit, flit, flit*. Puddles splashed up and soaked my pants. The cold, wet wind slapped my face. The knuckles of my hands were as red as raspberries.

Lucy Hiller lived on Merkle Stream Drive. I'd been there before, looking for a runaway bear. But that was a different case. I hoped this one didn't have any grizzly suspects with large teeth. I wasn't in the mood to be eaten.

Call me fussy.

Lucy had curly black hair, eyes like wet brown marbles, and wore red go-go boots.

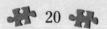 20

Lucy frowned when she saw me. "You're all wet."

"I took a shower with my clothes on," I replied. "It saves time."

Lucy grinned. "Come on in, Jigsaw. I'll see if my mom can make hot chocolate for us."

Ten minutes later we were alone at Lucy's kitchen table. "It's, um, about Bigs," Lucy began.

"Bigs Maloney," I murmured. The biggest, toughest, roughest kid in second grade. Just my luck. The guy ate nails for breakfast.

Lucy continued, "There's something going on with Bigs lately. I can't figure it out. He's been acting strange."

"Bigs Maloney has been acting strange since the day he was born," I joked.

Lucy didn't laugh.

I wrote in my detective journal:

CLIENT: LUCY HILLER

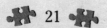 21

I looked out the rain-streaked window. The weather was so crummy it would even make a goldfish blue.

CASE: THE RAINY DAY MYSTERY

Lucy's eyes narrowed. "I think Bigs is up to something."

"Like what?"

"Like, um, I don't know," snapped Lucy.

"You're the detective, Jigsaw. Start detectin'!"

"That's not a lot to go on," I said. "He's acting strange. What else?"

Lucy twirled a finger through her curly locks. "Bigs used to come over on Tuesdays to play board games with me. But the last two weeks Bigs hasn't come. When I ask him why, Bigs won't give me a straight answer."

I took more notes, then closed my journal. "I can look around for clues," I said. "Maybe put a tail on him."

"A tail?" Lucy repeated.

"Spy," I answered. "Follow Bigs around for a few days. See what he's up to."

Lucy nodded thoughtfully.

I told Lucy it would cost her. "I get a dollar a day to make problems go away." I said. "This case won't be easy. Bigs is one tough cookie. I wouldn't want to get caught."

Lucy handed over three crisp dollar bills.

"Here's money to get you started," Lucy said. "I'll pay whatever it costs, Jigsaw."

We sealed the deal with a handshake.

"Let me ask you something, Lucy," I said. "Why do you care what Bigs Maloney does with his time?"

Lucy's face flushed pink. "That's my business," she said. "Your job is to do what I pay you to do."

Those pink cheeks told me a lot. Maybe, just maybe, Lucy had a crush on the big lug.

Chapter Five

Detective in Training

Joey came over after dinner. "I'm starving," he moaned. Joey swayed from side to side, as if dizzy with hunger.

I led him downstairs. "Okay, turn around and close your eyes." I placed a blindfold around his head.

"But I can't see," Joey protested.

"That's the idea," I explained.

I crept behind the washing

machine and pulled out a box. It was labeled:

It was where we kept our detective supplies. Walkie-talkies, fingerprint kits, disguises, a magnifying glass, rearview sunglasses — that kind of stuff. It was also where I stashed Joey's Twinkies.

"Okay, you can look now," I told Joey.

He pounced like he hadn't eaten in weeks. "That's enough," I said after watching him snarf down two Twinkies.

I pried the Twinkie box from Joey's hands. He cheered up when he spied my detective supplies. He tried on a green wig and a fake mustache. Joey put on a trench coat and a deerstalker cap. He played with my decoder ring, fiddled with my walkie-talkie, and studied a grape juice stain with a magnifying glass.

"Being a detective must be cool," he gushed.

"It's a living," I replied with a shrug.

And then I had an idea.

"Joey, are you free on Monday after school?"

"Yeah, why?" he asked.

I told him about my visit with Lucy Hiller. "I've got to spy on Bigs Maloney," I told him. "The problem is, I've got a dentist appointment after school on Monday."

I continued, "Following Bigs will be tricky. I can't do it all alone. And Mila is too sick to help. So how'd you like to be my right-hand man?"

"I'd love to, Jigsaw," Joey said. "But I can't."

"Why not?" I asked.

"I'm a lefty."

"So?"

Joey answered, "You said you want a right-hand man."

"I mean that I need a *helper*," I said. "Not a righty."

Joey, as usual, was confused. "So why didn't you say so in the first place?"

"I thought I did."

Joey shook his head. "Nuh-uh."

We made a deal. I'd hold on to Joey's Twinkies (there were eight left), and he would work with me for free.

"What do you want me to do?" Joey wondered.

I told Joey that I needed him to follow Bigs after school on Monday. "Keep your eyes open. See where he goes, watch what he does. That's it," I said. "Just put a tail on Bigs Maloney."

"Put a tail on Bigs Maloney," he repeated.

I stopped Joey on the way upstairs. "Hand it over," I ordered.

"Huh?"

"The Twinkie you slipped into your

pocket when you thought I wasn't looking,"
I said. "Hand it over."

Joey groaned. "Wow, you really are
ob-ser-ver-er-er-rer."

I couldn't argue with that.

Chapter Six

A Clue

Mila wasn't at the bus stop Monday morning. But Joey was there, pacing with excitement. "Are you ready for today?" I asked.

Joey patted his knapsack. "It's in the bag," he said.

Our classroom was room 201. Ms. Gleason was our teacher. We loved her. Even if she did pile on the homework sometimes.

I saw Bigs Maloney in the hallway. He was reading a book as he walked. "Hey, Bigs," I greeted him.

Bigs grunted like a big old bear. *Garrumph*.

"Strange," I said to Ralphie Jordan. "I don't remember Bigs being much of a reader."

Ralphie gave one of his big, toothy smiles. "Jigsaw, Bigs wants to be a professional wrestler when he grows up. I don't think I've *ever* seen him read a book."

"Well, I'm not sure he really *was* reading," I said. "Bigs was holding the book upside down!"

A scrap of paper fluttered to the ground behind Bigs. It was a bookmark with a picture of a puppy. There was a name scribbled on it:

LAURA LANE

The writing looked familiar. It was Bigs Maloney's handwriting. The sloppiest handwriting in room 201.

Right before morning recess I asked Joey to keep an eye on Bigs. It had stopped raining, so the class was going outside.

"Ms. Gleason asked me to stay in and help clean the hamster cage," I told Joey. "I'll be out later on."

After I finished with our hamsters, I wandered over to Bigs Maloney's desk. No one was around. I wanted to take a look at that book Bigs was reading. The cover showed that it was a G.I. Joe Adventure story. When I flipped through the pages, the words were upside down.

I checked the cover again. Just as I suspected. A phony cover had been taped over the book. I carefully peeled back the tape. Bigs wasn't reading a G.I. Joe Adventure — he was reading *The Baby-sitters Club*! He put on the phony cover so no one would know.

Lucy was right. Bigs *was* acting strange.

I looked through Bigs Maloney's

homework folder. Yep, the handwriting matched. He was definitely the one who wrote the name Laura Lane on the bookmark. Now, why would the big lug do that?

I knew a Patti Lane and a Sidney Lane. And, sure, there was Lois Lane — Superman's girlfriend. But I'd never heard of Laura Lane before.

I hurried outside and found Joey near

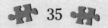

the swings. Bigs was on the other side of the playground, talking with Geetha Nair. That was weird, too. Bigs usually played soccer during recess.

I turned to Joey. "So, detective, did you learn anything while I was inside?"

Joey nodded happily. "Yes, two things." He held up a finger. "Number one, never stand in front of a swing if the person swinging on it has big feet." He rubbed his backside. "Youch."

"What else?"

Joey held up two fingers. "Number two, don't be fooled. Mud only *looks* like chocolate."

"Huh?"

"Bobby Solofsky tricked me," Joey complained. "He gave me a chocolate bonbon. So I gobbled it down. Only it wasn't chocolate. *Blech*."

I shook my head. "Joey, what about Bigs? Have you seen anything suspicious?"

"Nope, not really," he said. "But I'm all set to put a tail on Bigs, just like you asked."

"Don't let him see you," I warned once more.

"You can count on me, Jigsaw," Joey answered.

"That's what I'm afraid of," I said.

Chapter Seven
The Tail

Tailing a suspect is tricky business. When you follow someone, you have to stay close so you can see what's going on, but you can't get too close. You have to stay *out* of sight — while keeping the suspect *in* sight.

I worried about whether Joey could handle it.

I should have worried a lot more.

The first sign of "Bigs" trouble came after art class. Mr. Manus had brought in a special guest, an artist named Maria Rojas.

She came into the classroom holding a bunch of roses.

First we talked about roses for a long time. We had to use all scientific words, like petal and stamen and pollen.

Lucy Hiller raised her hand. "So, um, what's this got to do with painting?"

"Painting is about seeing," Ms. Rojas said. She placed a rose on each desk. "I want you to look at your rose very closely. Be *observant*. Count the petals, notice the shape of the stem and the jagged points on the leaves."

She continued, "Now I want you to paint it — using only the color pink."

"Pink?!" cried Eddie Becker. "That's my worst favorite color."

"I love pink," Danika Starling said.

"You would," Mike Radcliffe scoffed.

"Excuse me, Ms. Rojas," Mr. Manus said. "But why only pink?"

"I want the children to think about form and shape," Ms. Rojas answered. "And I want them to really explore what they can do using only one color."

We got right to work. After we finished, Ms. Rojas laid all our paintings on the floor. She made us look for things that were the same and different.

"It's amazing how different they are," Athena Lorenzo noted.

And she was right. I didn't know that painting was so much like detective work. You have to *observe* things closely. You have to look for little details. That's how a detective catches the bad guys. And it's how painters make their best art.

At the end of art class, we lined up to head back to our classroom. Ahead of me in the hallway, kids were snickering and laughing.

Joey rushed up to me, grinning happily. "I did it!" he whispered into my ear.

Then I saw what everyone thought was so funny. Bigs Maloney was walking ahead of us. He had a large cotton ball stuck to the seat of his pants.

Kids were laughing. They called out things like, "Have a *hoppy* day, Bigs!" and "What's up, doc?"

I turned to Joey. "You put a rabbit tail on Bigs Maloney's butt?!"

"With glue," Joey said.

"Why?"

"You told me to, Jigsaw."

"I did not," I said.

"Yes you did!" Joey argued. "You said, *'Put a tail on Bigs Maloney.'*"

"I didn't mean a fluffy bunny tail!" I

exclaimed. "I wanted you to *follow* him, Joey."

Joey frowned. "I was just trying to be your left-hand man."

I felt bad for Joey. It was an innocent mistake, I guess. "Sorry, Joey. It is sort of funny. But you better hope that Bigs doesn't find out."

Just then, an angry yell shook the walls. "Who did it?" Bigs Maloney hollered. He pointed wildly at everyone in sight. "Who thinks it's funny to make a bunny out of me?!

"I'LL CLOBBER THE BUM!"

Chapter Eight

Who Is Laura Lane?

Bigs stormed up to Joey. He laid a great paw on Joey's shoulder and snarled, "You bumped into me a few minutes ago. Is this your lousy idea of a prank?"

"Um . . . er . . ." Joey stammered.

Joey was about to beg for mercy. And I couldn't let that happen. I pulled the bookmark from my back pocket. "Hey, Bigs," I said. "Is this yours? I think you might have dropped it."

Bigs snatched the bookmark from my hand. "Yeah, that's mine."

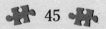

"Who is Laura Lane?" I asked.

"Huh? What are you talking about, Jones?" Bigs barked. He let go of Joey and stared down at me.

"There's a name on the bookmark," I pointed out. "Laura Lane. Is she a friend of yours?"

Bigs laughed in my face. "Very funny, Jones. It's none of your beeswax. Now, scram, both of you."

Bigs shook the cotton tail in his large fist. "If I find out you guys had something to do with this, I'll crush you like a couple of grapes."

And Bigs stormed away. Joey gulped.

After school I went to the dentist. Then I brought my aching gums to Mila's house. Ms. Gleason had asked me to drop off Mila's spelling homework.

It had started to rain again.

I showed up at Mila's carrying a closed umbrella. To be honest, I don't like umbrellas much. A hat is good enough for me. But this time, my umbrella was going to come in handy.

Mila was sitting in her living room, reading a book. A fuzzy blanket covered her legs.

"If it keeps on raining like this," I said, "I'm going to build an ark."

Mila laughed. "Like Noah, huh?"

"It feels like it's been raining for forty days and forty nights," I complained.

Mila started to hum, then sang softly:

"Who built the ark?
Jigsaw! Jigsaw!
Who built the ark?
Old Jigsaw built the ark!"

That was a good sign. Mila always sang when she was happy. And she always changed the words to the song. I noticed that Mila was fully dressed and, best of all, she looked a lot better.

"Your spots are almost gone," I said.

Mila grinned. "At least I don't look like a pizza anymore. My dad says I can go to school tomorrow."

"That's good news," I replied. "Joey has been helping me out. But he nearly got us killed by Bigs Maloney. I need you on this case, Mila."

I told her all about it. While I talked, Mila rocked back and forth. She said it was how she got her thinking machine started.

"I think the important clue is this Laura Lane person," I told Mila. "If we can find her, we might find out what Bigs has been up to."

"That name sounds familiar," Mila said. "I know a Patti Lane. . . ."

"And a Sidney Lane," I added.

"Did you check the school yearbook?" Mila asked.

"Um, not yet," I answered.

"How about the phone book?"

"Hey, give me a break," I complained. "I just spent the last half hour with Dr. Ackerman poking his fingers in my mouth. I can't do everything by myself."

"I guess you do need a partner," Mila said with a smile.

I guessed so.

"I'll look up Laura Lane later tonight,

after my homework," Mila promised. "There's definitely something familiar about that name."

I shrugged. "Maybe she's someone on your soccer team?"

Mila shook her head. "No, I don't think so. But don't worry, Jigsaw. I'll figure it out. Mila Yeh is back on the job!"

Chapter Nine

An Urgent Message

"First, let's test your brainpower," I said to Mila. "I have a secret message for you."

"Let me see!" Mila squealed.

"Not so fast," I said. "I hid it somewhere. And I'll give you a hint — it's not in my pockets."

Mila stared at me closely, from my soggy sneakers to my wet hat. "Under your hat," she guessed.

"Nope."

Mila pulled on her long black hair. "It's

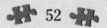

not like you to carry an umbrella," she noted. "Open it, please."

"But it's bad luck to open an umbrella in the house," I warned.

"I don't believe in that stuff," Mila answered. She grabbed the umbrella and *whoosh!* it flew open. A piece of paper was taped around the handle. Mila unwrapped the paper and smoothed it out on the table.

It read:

G ETW ELLSO ON DET ECTI VE!

Mila figured it out in less than a minute. "It's a space code," she said. "The words are all spelled the right way, but you put the spaces in the wrong places."

"An oldie but a goodie," I said.

Mila rewrote the message, but this time she took out all the spaces. Then she added slanted lines between the words, where the spaces should have been:

GET/WELL/SOON/DETECTIVE!

"I'm feeling better already." Mila laughed. *TCCCCHHH. BLIP. BUZZZZ. KA-CCCCHHH.*

"My walkie-talkie!" I exclaimed. I pulled it out of my pants pocket and pushed the TALK button. "Jigsaw Jones, over and out."

"Jigsaw, this is Joey!"

"I read you loud and clear," I said into the walkie-talkie.

"Bigs is — *ah-choo!* — on the move." Joey sniffled. "I've been following him — *ah-choo!* — all day. Bigs walked past Greenlawn Cemetery, down Willow Lane, up Fernbank Road. Now he's cutting through Sally Fields. *Ah-choo!*"

"Good work, Joey," I said. "And gesundheit."

"There's a problem, Jigsaw," Joey

whimpered, snorting through his nose. "I
have to — *ah-choo!* — go to the bathroom."

"Hold it," I said.

"But I really, *really*, REALLY have to go,"
Joey pleaded.

I rolled my eyes at Mila.

"Find out where Bigs is, *exactly*," Mila
whispered to me. She leaped to her feet
and pulled a map out from a desk.

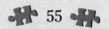

"Bigs is on Abbey Road, headed toward Brookside Drive," I repeated out loud.

Mila pointed to it on the map. "That's not far from here. Hurry, Jigsaw. Get your bike. You can catch up to Bigs if you pedal fast."

I looked out the window. The raindrops were the size of oranges.

I zipped up my raincoat (and sighed), pulled down my hat (and groaned), tightened my shoelaces (and sighed again).

"Wish me luck," I said.

And I raced out the door.

I had a date with a mud puddle and I couldn't be late.

Chapter Ten

Undercover

The street lamps were already lit — even though it was only late afternoon. The dark clouds and rain made it hard to see. At least the weather was working for me. In the rain, most people walked fast with their heads down. Bigs would be easy to follow.

Ahead of me, about one hundred feet away, I noticed something that looked like a large bear walking on the sidewalk. It was wearing a hooded N.Y. Giants raincoat. It could only be one person — Bigs Maloney.

I ditched my bike and followed the big

lug on foot. I zipped behind trees. Ducked behind parked cars. Sprinted forward, then dove beneath bushes.

That's when I slid and fell in the mud.

Yeesh!

I felt like a pig in a pigsty.

When I looked up, Bigs was gone.

I lifted my head and strained to see in all directions. Where did he go?

Somebody's porch light snapped on. The front door opened. Out stepped Bigs Maloney.

He was with Geetha Nair.

They stood talking on Geetha's porch. I could only hear the faint sound of voices, but no words. I had to get closer.

So I crawled like a snake through the slippery grass. It was risky, but I had to take the chance. A row of bushes hid me from view. Once I made it to the side of Geetha's house, I was okay.

Then I crawled closer and closer,

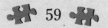

pressed against the front wall of Geetha's porch. I squatted behind a tall rosebush — ouch, thorns! I carefully pulled aside a branch, watched, and listened.

Geetha was holding a doll.

A baby doll in a diaper.

She handed it to Bigs. "Here's Poopsie," Geetha said. "Be nice to her."

Bigs tucked Poopsie under his coat.

You could have knocked me over with a Froot Loop.

"Thanks a lot," Bigs said. "I will."

Geetha was usually shy and rarely spoke above a whisper. I couldn't hear what she said next.

But Bigs boomed in his loud voice, "That's okay. I have diapers at home — the twins, you know."

Bigs Maloney? A doll and diapers? Twins?

Then I remembered. Bigs had twin brothers, Harry and Larry.

Ah-choo! I suddenly sneezed.

I held my hands over my face and froze in fear. Bigs glanced in my direction.

"Did you hear something?" he asked Geetha.

I sank as low to the ground as I could go. My heart climbed into my throat.

"Aw, musta' been the wind," Bigs said.

They said good-bye. Bigs hustled down the front walk, scrunching his shoulders against the wind and rain.

Thump, thump, thump.

My heart started beating again.

I considered that a good thing.

Then Geetha called out, "I'll see you at class on Tuesday! You remember where it is, don't you?"

Bigs turned in my direction. I made myself small behind the rosebush.

 62

It was a weird question to ask. *Of course* Bigs knew where class was. Good old room 201. He went there every day.

Bigs waved a slip of paper. "I won't get lost this time. I've got it written down right here."

That's when it hit me like a lightning bolt.

Bigs wasn't waving an ordinary piece of paper.

It was a bookmark.

The one that read LAURA LANE.

Chapter Eleven

Case Closed

Mila and I sat together on the bus Tuesday morning. The sun was shining brightly — and flowers suddenly seemed in bloom everywhere. "I couldn't find the name Laura Lane in the yearbook," Mila said. "And I called every Lane in the phone book."

"That's because Laura Lane isn't a person," I said.

"She's not?"

"Nope, she's a street!" I pulled out a local

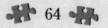

map. "See this little itty-bitty road? That's Laura Lane."

"Of course!" Mila exclaimed.

I told her everything I'd heard at Geetha's house.

"They must be taking some kind of class after school on Tuesdays," Mila guessed.

"Right." I nodded. "On Laura Lane. That's why Bigs wrote it down on his bookmark — so he wouldn't get lost."

We talked about the different clues. It was like laying out the pieces to a jigsaw puzzle. Bigs was reading a Baby-sitters Club book. He borrowed a baby doll from Geetha.

"He said he already 'had diapers at home," Mila added.

"That's what I don't get," I complained. "We've got all the pieces, but I don't see the picture."

"That's because you're a boy, Jigsaw."

"So?"

"So . . . think, Jigsaw," Mila said. "A mysterious class that Bigs doesn't want anyone to know about . . . a baby doll . . . diapers . . ."

"Yeah, what's he doing with that stuff?" I asked.

"Practicing," Mila answered.

Lucy sat in the seat in front of us. "Did you guys solve the case yet?" she asked.

"Almost," Mila promised.

The bus arrived at school. Mila grabbed me by the elbow. "Follow me, Jigsaw."

We found Geetha outside the main doors. "Hey, Geetha," Mila said. "Want to go Rollerblading after school today?"

Geetha smiled happily, then frowned. "I'd love to, except I have a class today after school."

"Oh, yeah," Mila said. "It's that baby-sitting thing, right?"

Geetha looked surprised. "Well, yes. We

have a test today. Hopefully I'll get my Mother's Helper Certificate."

"Does that make you an official baby-sitter?" Mila asked.

"Not really," Geetha answered. "I'm still too young for that. This means I'm trained to baby-sit, though. I learned a bunch of games and songs to play with kids, all kinds of safety stuff, even how to change diapers!"

"Cool!" Mila said. She gave me a sly wink.

"The class is on Laura Lane, right?" I asked.

Geetha looked surprised again. "Right," she said. "How did you know?"

"It's my job to know things," I replied with a shrug.

lunch, Mila and I sat across from my client, Lucy Hiller. I reported my findings.

"Isn't that sweet!" Lucy gushed. "Bigs is taking a baby-sitting class."

"I guess he didn't want anyone to know," I said. "Guys like Solofsky would make fun of him."

Lucy nodded. "Thanks, Jigsaw. I guess Bigs wasn't acting so strange after all."

I didn't know about that. It was strange to think of the biggest, roughest, toughest kid in the whole grade changing diapers. But you have to make money somehow. And not everyone can be a detective. Besides, Bigs does have two baby brothers. He'd probably be doing a lot of baby-sitting over the next few years.

"You owe me another dollar," I told Lucy. "I had to hire some help."

Mila and I found Joey sitting at a table with Ralphie Jordan and Eddie Becker. Joey had just set a new record by eating two bologna sandwiches in under eight seconds. Ralphie and Eddie looked thrilled. Joey, on the other hand, looked a little green around the gills.

I handed Joey a dollar bill. "Here's a portrait of our first president," I said. "You did good work, Joey. Consider it a bonus. Thanks."

Joey smiled from ear to ear. "Cool, now I'm a real detective!" he exclaimed.

"Well, not exactly," I said. "Consider yourself a Detective's Helper."

Then I handed Joey a small paper bag.

"What's this?" he wondered.

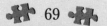

"I figured you could use a couple of Twinkies," I said.

"Thanks, Jigsaw!" Joey said. He gave me a high five. "You're the best."

"Maybe," I said. I looked at Mila, then at Joey, and winked. "But I got a little help from my friends."